SADIE

SADIE

BY

CHERYL LYNN WEAMS

XULON PRESS

Xulon Press
2301 Lucien Way #415
Maitland, FL 32751
407.339.4217
www.xulonpress.com

Paperback ISBN-13: 978-1-6628-4071-5
Ebook ISBN-13: 978-1-6628-4072-2

Table of Contents

Chapter 1

The church service started at 11:00a.m. Good old down south foot stomping hand clapping gospel music could be heard coming from the church. The choir was singing, "His Eye is on the Sparrow" and Sadie Ward and her parents Jim and Sara were sitting in the service. Sara stood up clapping her hands and enjoying church when she noticed that Sadie had fallen asleep.

"Sadie! Sadie! Wake up, girl!! What is the matter with you? You know better than that. You shouldn't fall asleep in church," Sara chided. Jim tapped his hand on Sadie's shoulder and looked at her with disappointed eyes.

"Wake up, Sadie," Jim whispered. As Jim was talking to Sadie, he shoved her harder trying to wake her up. Sara noticed that Jim was a little loud.

"You two need to be quiet!!! I mean right now!!! Do you realize that you are in church?" Sara faced Jim and Sadie with her eyebrows raised.

"I know, Sara," Jim whispered. "Sadie fell asleep, and I'm trying to wake her up." Sara turned toward Sadie and pointed her finger.

"Girl, you know better than that!! You better not let that happen again or I will take you outside and spank you," Sara said with authority. Sara, disappointed with Sadie, was trying to focus her attention back to the church service.

Sadie responded, “Yes mamma,” and turned her attention to the singing choir while Sara and Jim turned back to the service, standing and clapping their hands. , Sadie listened to the choir as Sister Green sang the solo part of the song.. “Boy, she can really sing!! I pray that one day when I grow up, I will be able to sing just like Sister Green,” Twelve-year-old Sadie thought as she heard the notes ring out strong and vibrant.

Chapter 2

Fifteen years had passed since the Sunday church scene. Fifteen years since Sadie innocently fell asleep in church and woke to hear the beautiful choir singing., To Sadie, now twenty-seven years old, it seemed like a lifetime ago. Sadie's parents had since died, and she was now living with her Aunt Neisse.

Sadie was not happy about living with her Aunt Neisse because of Neisse's lifestyle and the harsh treatment Sadie received from her. Sadie had attended Unify College for one year but had to stop to help with bills and food. She had gotten a job working at Press Cleaners which was down the street from where they lived. The majority of the time, Aunt Neisse would take Sadie's money and gamble and drink all night long.

It was Easter Sunday morning and Sadie was getting ready for church. She thought about asking Aunt Neisse to go with her even though she knew that church was not something Aunt Neisse was interested in attending.

"Aunt Neisse, you should go to church with me today. It's Easter Sunday, Sadie asked hoping the holiday might entice her to come.

Aunt Neisse responded with a chuckle, "Who me? Girl, I have a date tonight and it's gonna take me all day to get ready for it. I just met this new dude at the club last night and he wants to take me out."

Sadie pressed on, "Oh come on, Aunt Neisse!! Just this one Sunday! Please? I am singing today, and I guarantee you would enjoy the service".

"Well Sadie, you know I just love to hear you sing. Let me think about it for a moment," Aunt Neisse said softly. Aunt Neisse turned away as if she was in deep thought.

"Okay, Sadie, I guess it won't hurt to go especially since it's Easter Sunday, but I have one condition! We must leave early so I can get ready for my date tonight," Aunt Neisse said with a smile.

"All right, Aunt Neisse, I promise you will not regret it," Sadie gushed with excitement. Sadie reached out to give Aunt Neisse a hug.

Even though Sadie did not always like living with Aunt Neisse, she did appreciate having her in her life. She knew that her aunt did the best that she could, and Sadie loved her in spite of how she treated her at times.

"Auntie, I love you so much and I thank you for taking care of me for all these years after mamma died. I don't know what I would do without you," Sadie told her.

Aunt Neisse started to cry, "Yeah, baby, I miss my sister so much!! She wouldn't have it any other way."

Chapter 3

At Mt. Calvary Baptist Church the choir was always singing and Sadie was the lead vocalist. Fifteen years after Sadie prayed to grow up to sing like Sister Green, it was an answered prayer. The choir was singing, and the audience was rejoicing, shouting, and praising God. While Sadie was singing, the audience was in an uproar, shouting. The church was full, standing room only. When the song ended Pastor Ray started talking about the goodness of God.

Pastor Ray started talking in his distinct preacher's voice, "Good morning, church!! Praise the Lord. This is the day that the Lord has made, now let us rejoice and be glad in it. I tell you, every time Sister Sadie Ward sings, the Holy Spirit just has His way! Say amen, church." The church responded with scattered "amens", head shakes, and waving hands. They all knew Sadie's singing was special. Pastor Ray shared the Word of God with the congregation before ending with announcements.

"Now, I got up to remind you all of our church picnic next Sunday afternoon. Hope to see you all there. May God bless and keep you until we meet again. Let us all stand and be dismissed," Pastor Ray concluded.

Church had ended and everyone was surrounded around Sadie when Eddie King walked up to her.

"Miss Sadie, Miss Sadie! Wow, girl, you can really blow. I've never heard anyone sing the way you do. Your voice is out of this world. Thank you for sharing your gift," Eddie shook his head in amazement.

"All the glory goes to God," Sadie replied with a humble smile.

"Yeah, you can say that again, Sadie."

Sadie had not seen Eddie at church before, so she asked, "Is this your first time at the church?"

"Yeah, my first time but surely not my last. I will definitely be back." Eddie turned to go but hesitated. Sadie could sense he wanted to say more. Turning back around Eddie continued, "Sadie, do you think I could get your phone number?"

Sadie was surprised he would be so bold. She stammered, "Well, I don't know."

Eddie smiled as Sadie's confusion registered. He chuckled ,"Oh, do you think I'm asking you out? Oh no. Sorry. Sadie, I'm a talent agent, and I was wondering if you would be interested in coming to my studio to record."

Sadie was stunned! "Record Me!! Do you think I am good enough?"

Eddie paused and smiled a sincere smile, "Sadie, you are better than good. Girl, the world needs to hear you."

Sadie was still in disbelief. Was this even real? She tried to sound confident, "Well I don't know, Mr. uh,"

"Eddie, just call me Eddie."

"Well Eddie, I really don't know. You know I just met you and now days you have to be careful and..."

Eddie reassured her, "Sadie, I am really an honest guy and I just want to help you get ahead in life and let the world hear your great voice. I tell you what, do I need to talk to your parents first?"

The mention of her parents always pierced Sadie's heart. She responded matter of fact, "My parents are deceased, and I live with my aunt for right now."

Eddie looked sympathetic, "Well perhaps we need to talk to your aunt before you make a decision."

Sadie was a little insulted. She was not a teenager. She was a responsible adult. "I make my own decisions; I am grown."

Eddie smiled, "So you are grown. Okay, Ms. Sadie, I like that. I like a woman who makes her own decisions." Sadie studied Eddie's face. Was he for real? She couldn't tell.

Eddie reached into his pocket, "Well look, here's my card. Give me a call on tomorrow and maybe we can set up something."

He started to walk away and then looked over his shoulder and playfully said, "Hope I hear from you soon. Don't make me wait, Ms. Sadie. I have many clients, and I am looking for someone next week with a great voice like yours to come into my studio free of charge."

Sadie tried to keep her excitement inside, but she couldn't, "Free!! Are you serious! You mean I don't have to pay anything?"

"That's right, Sadie. Everything is on me. Call me, okay?" Eddie said. This time he looked more serious.

Sadie replied, "Okay, I'll think about it."

Eddie walked towards her and almost whispered, "Just don't take too long". He touched her chin, turned, and walked away.

Sadie stood there in shock wondering what she should do. Her best friend Sissy walked over to see why Sadie was just standing there gazing.

"Sadie? Sadie?" Sissy waved her hand across Sadie's face, "Sadie, girl what is wrong with you?"

Sadie snapped out of it, "Sissy, this guy just told me that he is a talent agent, and he wants me to record in his studio."

Sissy looked doubtful. After all, this kind of stuff just doesn't happen. "Really girl? You got to be kidding."

"No, I'm not kidding. It's true." Sadie handed the card to Sissy, "See, here's his number." Sissy read the card out loud, "Stardom Studio We Make Stars to Shine. Girl, I cannot believe it."

Sadie wanted to know what her best friend thought. "I can't either. What do you think about it, Sissy?

Sissy put her arm around Sadie, "I think we should go down there and check it out."

"We?" Sadie smiled and raised her eyebrows.

"Yes we, girl," Sissy laughed, "Hey, I can be your background singer." Sissy started singing as her and Sadie left the church and went out to lunch.

After lunch, Sadie went home to relax and think about her encounter with Eddie. Sadie decided she wasn't going to wait to call Eddie. She was excited and curious. She picked up the card and called Eddie. The phone only rang once when she heard, "Speak to me!!"

Sadie stammered, "Uh, yes, may I speak to Mr. Eddie, oh I mean Eddie?"

Eddie responded harshly, "Who is this? I don't have time to play games with you. Mean what you say and say what you mean."

Sadie hung up the phone. She was already scared and nervous, but Eddie's response made her question everything. If that even was Eddie. Did she dial the wrong number? It sounded like him, but he was not as sweet as he had been at church.

The phone rang while Sadie was still trying to figure out what happened.

Sadie, "Hello?"

"Yeah, did you just call this number?" the voice asked.

Sadie, "Yes, is this Stardom Studio?"

The voice was still a little harsh, "Yes, it is and who are you?"

"This is Sadie," Sadie said awkwardly.

Immediately the voice softened, and Sadie recognized it was Eddie, "Oh Sadie, why didn't you say so? The girl with the golden voice. I'm sorry I didn't know it was you. How are you ?"

"I'm fine. Did I catch you at a bad time?" Sadie felt relieved that Eddie sounded sweet again but also hesitant. Did she call too soon?

"No, darling, I have all the time in the world for you," Eddie answered sweet as honey.

Sadie smiled, "Well I was wondering…well, if you were still interested in me recording at your studio?"

Eddie responded, "Sure, baby. I am very interested. I tell you what, can you come by the studio tomorrow say around 7:00p.m."

Sadie thought she would ask one more time, "Are you serious?"

"Yeah baby, I am very serious."

Sadie took a deep breath and let it out slowly, "Okay, just give me the directions and I will be there. Eddie explained that the studio was located on the corner of Wilkins and Holland behind Shop and Stop.

Sadie confirmed the appointment, "All right I will be there tomorrow at 7:00p.m."

"Later baby, looking forward to seeing you. Sweet dreams," Eddie said, his voice sweet and calming

Chapter 4

Eddie hung up the phone and looked up to see his friend Foster staring down at him. "Hey man, who you trying to con this time," Foster laughed. He knew Eddie's game all too well.

Eddie defended himself, "No man, this girl can really sing. We can make a lot of money off her. Trust me on this one."

Foster shook his head, "Man you know what happened last time. It was a disaster".

"I know but just trust me on this one. This girl is green, straight from Sunny Brook Farm, if you know what I mean. I have a plan," Eddie answered confidently.

The next night Sadie and Sissy were getting ready to go to the studio. Aunt Neisse walked into the room just as they were finishing.

Aunt Neisse gave them a skeptical look, "And where do you two think you're going? Sadie, you didn't tell me you were going out. And by the way, where is the money for your half of the rent?"

Sadie could not hide her frustration, "Aunt Neisse, I gave you money last week. What did you do with that money?"

"I spent the money on the light and telephone bill and oh by the way, I do have to feed you," Aunt Neisse shot back

"Look, Aunt Neisse, I gave you all the money that I had last week. You have taken every cent from me. I don't have any more money!" Sadie knew this conversation would end with a guilt trip, but she had to stand up for herself. She loved Aunt Neisse but she was growing tired of the same conversation over and over.

"Girl, I know you're not raising your voice at me. I will take this shoe off and knock you upside your head. Don't you know that I feed you and take care of you?" Sadie braced herself. She knew what was next.

Aunt Neisse continued, "Shoot if it wasn't for me, you wouldn't have a place to live. I took you in when your mamma died!" To emphasize her point, Aunt Neisse started crying, "Oh my poor sister is gone, oh Lord." Sadie grabbed her purse and handed Aunt Neisse fifty dollars.

Sadie didn't know if it was the chance she was taking by meeting with Eddie, but at that moment she felt bold and decided to say what she had been wanting to say to Aunt Neisse. "Here. This is my last fifty dollars, take it. I know what you really do with all the money. I heard about you out there clubbing and drinking. And to be honest, Aunt Neisse, you too old for that."

"You don't tell me what to do and don't you talk to me that way. If you don't like how things are here, then you can just leave," Aunt Neisse shouted.

Sadie was not fazed. She knew that she had to speak her mind, "You know what? Maybe I will. I need my own place anyway."

Aunt Neisse was fuming, "You little ungrateful brat."

Sadie was letting it all out now. She was not holding back, "Ungrateful? You are the one that is ungrateful. Ever since my parents died I have taken care of myself.

I have worked every day and I'm the one who looks out for me, not you.". . Sadie grabbed her purse and left.

Aunt Neisse yelled after her, "Run you little brat; you'll be back, I guarantee it. Aunt Neisse laughed and counted the money while she made plans to go to the club. As she stood there, the lights shut off. "What is going on!! I thought I paid my bill!!" She ran to the phone and the phone was disconnected. "Oh lord, now what am I going to do?" Aunt Neisse put her head in her hands contemplating what she was going to do when there was a knock on the door. Aunt Neisse was sure Sadie was back to apologize but when she opened the door, she saw Ralph the local drug dealer.

"Hey woman, I told you I am not waiting all night for you; now come on.". Ralph looked around, "Girl, why are the lights off? You trying to impress old Ralph? Come here, baby."

Aunt Neisse was not in the mood for Ralph's jokes, "Man get out of the way!! My lights just got cut off and Sadie left. But she will be back. You can bet on that."

Chapter 5

Sadie and Sissy arrived at the studio. Sissy looked at Sadie concerned," Sadie, girl, what are you going to do? You told Aunt Neisse you were done and now you don't have a place to go. You know you could come and stay with me, but you know how it is, girl, too many people at my house and we just don't have any room. Sorry."

Sadie shrugged her shoulders, "Don't worry about it. The Lord will make a way somehow."

Sadie took a deep breath, squeezed Sissy's hand and knocked on the door. Foster opened the door and broke into a wide smile, "Hello ladies. What can I do for you?"

Sadie was surprised to see someone other than Eddie, "Uh, my name is Sadie Ward, and I am looking for Eddie.

Foster smiled even wider, "So, you're Sadie. Come on in. I've been expecting you. I'm Foster. Eddie told me all about you and he said that you can really sing. Would you ladies like a drink?"

This was not what Sadie expected, "Oh, no thank you."

"Eddie is not here right now. He will be back shortly. We can go ahead and get started if that is ok with you," Foster explained

Sadie wasn't exactly sure about Foster, but Sissy gave her a little push, "Uh, sure, no problem."

Foster showed Sadie to the sound room. He showed her the list of backtracks available and she picked one she knew. She put the headphones on and started singing.

Foster was blown away, "Man, girl, Eddie was right! You can really sing. You are amazing. You're going to blow up, girl."

Sadie could not believe this was happening, "You really think so?"

"Yeah, trust me. You are going to be a star soon," Foster said.

Sadie looked at Sissy, "Did you hear that, Sissy, a star?"

Sissy whispered in Sadie's ear, "Yeah girl. Now tell him I can sing too."

"Later, Sissy, I'll tell him later," chuckled Sadie.

Eddie walked in the room applauding Sadie, "That was fantastic, girl. I told you. Just a matter of time and you will be a famous recording artist." Eddie looked at Foster, "Foster, I told you, man."

Foster shook his head, "Yeah, she is great, man."

Eddie turned towards Sadie, "Now, I tell you what, Sadie, let me call a few people tonight and let them listen to your track and then I will get back with you tomorrow."

This was all happening so fast. Sadie replied, "Okay, that will be fine with me." Sadie paused for a few seconds and then continued, "Eddie, do you think I can make it to the top?"

"What!!! Girl, in my eyes you are already a star." Eddie grabbed Sadie's chin, "Just trust me." Sadie smiled and then she noticed that Foster and Sissy were in the corner talking and laughing. Sissy called across the room, "Hey, Sadie, I'll be back in a few minutes. Just going for a little ride."

Sadie walked over to Sissy and grabbed Sissy's hand, "Sissy, can I talk to you for a moment?" Sadie led Sissy to the other side of the room "Girl, where are you going? You hardly know that guy and besides you know I don't have a place to stay right now. I need to go home with you."

Sissy smiled, "Just stay here until I get back. I won't be gone long, okay? Girl, this dude is cute." Sissy let go of Sadie's hand and walked to the door where Foster was waiting. Sadie yelled, "Sissy, Sissy wait!!!" But Sissy left out the door with Foster leaving her and Eddie standing there.

"Would you like for me to take you home?" Eddie asked.

"Oh no thanks. I'm gonna ride the bus," Sadie responded, grabbing her purse and heading towards the door.

Eddie scoffed, "The bus? Don't be silly. It's too late to be talking about riding the bus. Besides I don't want anything to happen to my little star now." Eddie smiled and walked towards Sadie, "I tell you what, I'll just give you a ride home. Okay? Sadie tried to hold it in, but she couldn't. She started crying putting her face in her hands.

Eddie's faced looked concerned, "What's wrong, baby? Did I say something wrong?"

"Oh no, Eddie, that's not it. I had an argument with my aunt, and I left. Now I don't have a place to go," Sadie explained.

Eddie hugged Sadie, "Hey don't cry, everything is going to be ok. You can stay at my apartment until you get on your feet."

Sadie pulled back, "I don't really know you and I don't think it's a good idea."

"Oh no, baby," Eddie is laughed, "Do you think I'm making some kind of move? I'm just trying to help you out. You can sleep in my bed, and I will sleep on the couch. Hey, I respect you, and I would not do anything to harm you."

Sadie was hesitant, "Are you sure?"

"Yes, I'm positive, Eddie said, "Just trust me." It seemed like Eddie said to trust him a lot but what choice to Sadie have. She could wait there for Sissy, take the bus, or take Eddie up on his offer. She didn't really like any of those choices, "Well I guess it will be all right until tomorrow. I have to be at work tomorrow at 8:00a.m."

Eddie put his hand on her shoulder, "Okay I will make sure that I will have you there on time under one condition!!"

Sadie glanced at him squinting her yes, "And what is that?"

"If you would have dinner with me tonight. I am hungry!! I know you have to be hungry after all that good singing," Eddie said.

Sadie smiled, "Well, I guess I am a little hungry". Eddie and Sadie left the studio and went to a nearby restaurant and then to Eddie's apartment.

Eddie unlocked the door and held it open for Sadie to walk in, "Well did you enjoy the food?"

"Yes, it was very good, and the place was cozy too. Do you go there often?" Sadie replied

"Not that often but I try to go every chance I get because it's so good. Can I get anything for you? A glass of wine, water, or coffee?" Eddie asked while walking into the kitchen.

Sadie looked around taking in the details of Eddie's apartment, "No thank you. I'm fine".

Eddie mumbled under his breath, "Yeah you can say that again."

Sadie turned around to face Eddie, "Did you say something?"

"Oh no just said I'm glad we are friends," Eddie lied.

"Oh. You have a very nice apartment. I'm sure your girlfriend likes it. I hope you don't get in trouble by having me over here," Sadie said as she looked around the apartment more.

"Sadie, you need to relax. I have everything under control. I tell you what, let me fix you a glass of wine so you can relax your mind," Eddie replied smoothly.

"Oh, I don't think so," Sadie said. She didn't really want to drink

Eddie coaxed her, "Come on, a little glass of wine isn't going to hurt you."

Sadie smiled shyly, "Okay, just a little though. I have to go to work in the morning. Eddie brought Sadie a glass and wine and made a toast, "To the future!!"

Sadie took a sip, "This is bitter, and I don't like it."

Eddie rolled his eyes, "You're so worried. Just relax, Sadie." Sadie drank the rest of her wine and fell asleep on the couch. Eddie covered her with a blanket and turned the lights out.

Chapter 6

The next day Sadie woke up and realized it was 10:00a.m. Sadie let out a screech, "Oh no, oh no!! I overslept!!!I can't believe it!!!" Eddie ran into the living room, "What's wrong, Sadie?"

Sadie threw the blanket off her and grabbed her purse, "I overslept and now I am late for work. I'm gonna be in so much trouble."

Eddie laughed, "Just calm down, Sadie, calm down. I'll take you to work. Calm down. I told you that wine was going to relax you."

"It's not funny, Eddie. I can lose my job," Sadie shot back in a panic.

"Okay, okay, Sadie. I was just kidding," Eddie said while grabbing his keys and walking to the door. They left the house and drove to Press Cleaners. Eddie walked Sadie to the door and asked, "Are you okay, now? I told you to just trust me."

Sadie sighed, "Thank you so much, Eddie, for everything."

Eddie kissed Sadie lightly on the cheek, "You are welcome. I will call you this afternoon. Good-bye." Sadie walked inside and the manager, Jeff met Sadie at the door, "Sadie, you're late again!!! And not just a little bit late but two hours!!! Girl, I have given you too many chances and you blew it this time. I have to let you go. You're fired, Sadie."

Sadie started crying, "Jeff, please I really need my job. Please give me another chance, please."

Jeff shook his head, "I'm sorry, Sadie I knew this was coming and I've already hired another person in your place."

"Jeff, please give me another chance I'm begging you; I really need my job," Sadie sobbed.

"I'm sorry, Sadie. It's too late," Jeff said as he walked her out the door. Sadie walked away with her head down, crying and upset only to look up and see Eddie. She ran right into his arms.

Eddie looked confused, "What's wrong? You left your purse in my car and I was…" Sadie responded before he could finish explaining, "Eddie, I just got fired."

Before Eddie could respond, Sissy ran up to Sadie, "Girl, let me tell you about my night. What's wrong? Why are you crying?"

Sadie was not in the mood to hear about Sissy's night. Her leaving is what got Sadie in this situation in the first place, "Not now, Sissy, I just got fired."

Sissy's jaw dropped, "Fired? What happened? You know, Jeff is crazy, girl. Do you want me to go in there and tell him off? You know I will".

Sadie snapped at Sissy, "Just forget about it. Forget about it!!!"

"Girl, he is wrong for doing that to you. What are you going to do? You have no money and no place to go! You can't go back after how you talked to Aunt Neisse. You're homeless. What are you going to do?" Sissy's voice escalated with panic.

Sadie yelled, "Calm down, Sissy!!! You know what? Just be quiet. You are making matters worse.

Eddie stepped between Sadie and Sissy, "Sadie, you can come stay with me for a while until you get on your feet. I'll let you use my car to look for a job. Don't worry. Everything will be all right, just trust me."

Sadie wasn't sure. She was used to taking care of herself, "Oh I don't know. I really don't want to be a bother to anyone."

Eddie caressed her arm, "Sadie, I'm your friend now and I'm just trying to help a friend out."

"Okay. I guess it will be okay but only until I get on my feet," Sadie said feeling relieved.

Eddie touched her chin, "Now let me see that beautiful smile." Sadie smiled and let Eddie led her to the car.

Chapter 7

After two weeks of looking for a job, Sadie found one at Gray's Diner. The job didn't pay a lot, but Sadie was back on her feet again and she was very happy. Sadie's supervisor, Jerome Gray had a crush on Sadie and things were getting a little out of hand.

"Good morning, Mr. Gray!!" Sadie said cheerfully as she walked in the door.

"Good morning, Sadie, how are you today?" Jerome asked.

Sadie smiled, "I am wonderful. The birds are singing, the flowers are blooming, and I am on top of the world."

"Sadie, you know I've wanted to tell you something for a good while now. I really like having you around here. You have made the business grow and we have more customers than we ever had before," Jerome explained.

Sadie was shocked, "Are you serious, Mr. Gray?

Jerome got close to Sadie, "Yes, I am very serious. You know you are really a beautiful young lady, and I would like to ask you ..."

Jerome couldn't finish what he wanted to say because Eddie walked into the restaurant. "Hey, good morning ya'll!!" Jerome walked away leaving Sadie standing there nervous and trembling.

"Hey, Eddie? What are you doing here so early?" Sadie asked trying to stop the tremble in her voice.

Eddie laughed, "Well, can't a man have some breakfast? And besides, I got some good news, Sadie."

Sadie tuned towards Eddie, "Good news? What is it, Eddie? What's the good news?"

Eddie stretched trying his best to act casual, "Well, Sadie, I signed you up with a record label."

"What!! I cannot believe Are you serious?" Sadie said overwhelmed with shock.

"I told you, Sadie. I told you to just trust me. Girl, you're on your way to Hollywood," Eddie said. Sadie hugged Eddie, "Thank you, thank you so much, Eddie."

Eddie lifted her chin so he could look her in the eyes, "You did all the work, I just assisted. We have a lot of work to do so when you get done with work, we need to go to the studio."

Sadie bounced on her feet, "Okay, okay. Eddie. I will be there after I get off work." Eddie and Sadie did not realize that Jerome was standing in the back listening to their conversation, and he wasn't happy.

"You know, baby, one day you will be able to leave this nickel and dime job and make some real money. I saw how close that dude was up on you. What's really going on?"

Sadie shook her head, "He is just my boss. What are you talking about?"

Eddie's jaw clenched, "Yeah well, you just make sure that doesn't happen again. I don't like him."

Sadie didn't know what came over him, "Eddie, please stop being silly."

Eddie got close to Sadie and grabbed her arm, "I told you, I don't want him touching you again. Do you understand?"

Sadie was uncomfortable and just wanted him to leave, "Yeah, Eddie, I understand." Eddie grabbed his hat and started walking out. Before he left, he turned around and said, "Don't keep me waiting too long, Sadie, we have a lot of work to do."

Sadie was standing there in shock wondering what had just happened when Jerome came from the back of the restaurant. "Sadie, you don't have to put up with that. He shouldn't talk to you that way," Jerome said sounding concerned.

"He didn't mean anything by that. He was just kidding around," Sadie felt like she had to defend Eddie even though she didn't understand why he had acted that way.

Jerome continued, "Yeah, I bet he was kidding. Sadie, listen, I have seen guys like that before… you need to be careful."

"I will be all right," Sadie answered feeling confused, "Look we got customers coming, I better get to work.

Sadie's shift ended at five. She was sitting at the table counting her tips while Jerome was cleaning up and sweeping the floor.

Jerome looked over at Sadie, "Sadie, girl, looks like you made a lot of tips today."

Sadie smiled, "Yes, I made two hundred dollars in tips." Sadie started singing The Lord is Blessing Me Right Now.

Sadie heard the door open and looked up to see Aunt Neisse walking in. Sadie wondered how she knew where she was working. Aunt Neisse smiled, "Girl, I've been looking everywhere for you." Sadie knew from her slurred speech and stumbling into chairs that Aunt Neisse was intoxicated. "Girl, I've been looking everywhere for you," she repeated. "What you doing, Sadie? You look so good. Look at you! The spitting image of your mother."

Sadie was embarrassed and she felt her face flush. Why did Aunt Neisse have to do this to her at her job? Jerome already thought Sadie had problems with Eddie.

Aunt Neisse continued her drunken speech, "Sadie, Sadie, Sadie, girl, auntie needs a huge favor. I need to pay my light bill. I don't know where else to go or who to turn to. Ralph left me, Sadie, and I don't have anybody else." Aunt Neisse had made her way to Sadie's side and was now crying on Sadie's shoulder. " Sadie, please, please help me out. I promise I will pay you back as soon as I get back on my feet. I'm going to get myself together and pay you all your money back."

Sadie pushed Aunt Neisse off her shoulder, "How did you find me? How did you know that I worked here?"

Aunt Neisse wiped her eyes on her sleeve, "I heard about it on the streets. Do you have a problem with me knowing where you work? You don't want to help your favorite auntie out? I took care of you when..."

Sadie interrupted her, "I know the story, Aunt Neisse. You don't have to keep telling me that. Here, take this money and pay your light bill." Sadie handed Aunt Neisse some of her tips.

"Thank you, sweetheart, thank you. I will pay you back I promise." Aunt Neisse left the restaurant stumbling and falling along the way. Ralph was waiting for her outside.

"How much did you get, woman?" Ralph asked.

"Fifty dollars!!" Aunt Neisse said proudly.

Ralph was not impressed, "That's all?" Ralph slapped Aunt Neisse. "That's what you had last time. You better get my money or I will kill you and your little niece. Now you know what you need to do. Go and make my money," Ralph screamed in her face.

Jerome walked out from the back shaking his head, "Girl, your aunt has real problems. She needs some help"

"I know Jerome. She has been that way since my mother died. I really believe that she has lost all of her self-esteem and she just doesn't care about life anymore. She used to be a lawyer and she was disbarred for having drugs in her system. It's just a waste. She needs to get her life together and give God some of her time. You know what, Mr. Gray? She taught me how to sing. She has a great talent, and she is letting it go to waste. It makes me sad," Sadie frowned. "Well, my bus is coming I better go now," Sadie said while she gathered her tips and started towards the door.

"Sadie, do you need a ride home? I don't mind dropping you off," Jerome said kindly.

"No thank you. I am going to catch the bus." Sadie said.

"Okay, just know that I am here for you if you need anything." Jerome added.

"I know, Mr. Gray, I know. See you tomorrow." Sadie waved as she left.

Chapter 8

Sadie arrived at the studio. Foster and Eddie were in the studio listening to some music. Eddie stood up, "Hey, what took you so long? I told you we have a lot of work to do and you are just messing around taking your own sweet time. We got to make some money."

Sadie was annoyed, "Is that what it is all about, Eddie? Making money?"

"As a matter of fact, it is. Now stop wasting time and let's lay these tracks down." Eddie snapped.

"Okay, Eddie, you're the boss," Sadie said sarcastically.

"That's right I am the boss and if it weren't for me, you wouldn't have a place to live," Eddie shot back. Sadie held her head down and kept her mouth closed. She did owe Eddie a lot. After she finished singing, Eddie gave her a hug and a kiss on the cheek.

"Now that's my girl! girl you are bad. I liked that because you were singing with feeling. I guess I need to make you mad all the time," Eddie said laughing. Foster was laughing too. Sadie didn't like when they laughed at her.

"Hey, Sadie, I'm hungry. Let's go down to The Grubb and get something to eat," Eddie said, grabbing his coat. Sadie went with him hoping he would be nicer once he wasn't so hungry. Sadie and Eddie were just getting their food when one of Eddie's girls walked in.

"Hey Eddie, what is going on, baby?" she said sweetly. She looked at Sadie and said, "Hey, how you doing?" When Eddie didn't respond, she looked at him and said, "Eddie you act like you don't know me. I'm your number one girl, remember?"

Eddie was mad, "You need to leave!! You can see I'm having dinner with someone."

"Okay, Eddie, I will remember that. I know you're trying to ignore me, but that's all right."

"Man, I tell you, you can take them out of the country, but you can't take the country out of them," Eddie shook his head, "Sorry about that, Sadie."

Sadie shrugged, "It's ok. Who was that?"

"Uh, uh, just a longtime friend, that's all," Eddie stammered.

Sadie pressed him, "Did you go to high school together?"

"Yeah, yeah, we went to high school together," Eddie answered. After they finished eating, they left the restaurant to go back to Eddie's apartment.

"I am exhausted. I think I am going to bed early tonight," Sadie said yawning.

Eddie was not having it, "Bed? You know we need to celebrate."

"Celebrate!! Celebrate what? I worked all day long and had to give all my money to my crack head aunt," Sadie said.

Eddie clenched his fists, "What? What? She took your money, Sadie? What did you let her do that for?"

Sadie tried to explain, "She said that she needed to pay a bill, so I let her have it."

"Girl, I need to teach you how to stand up for yourself. Anyway, let me get you a glass a wine before you go to bed," Eddie said, heading to the kitchen.

"I don't think so. I really just want to go to bed," Sadie answered headed towards the bathroom.

Eddie wasn't giving up, "Hey, it will help you sleep. I promise I will wake you up for work tomorrow."

Sadie sighed, "Fine, I guess a little won't hurt." Eddie handed her a glass of wine and Sadie kept drinking and drinking until she was drunk. She started singing and playing around with Eddie. She sat on his lap, and they started kissing. Eddie picked her up and took her into the bedroom.

Chapter 9

One month later, Sadie was singing in night clubs and making money for Eddie only. Sadie was on stage, and she was exhausted from lack of rest. The song was over, and Sadie was at the bar ordering a drink.

"Hey, Sam, hit me again with another cognac straight up," Sadie said.

"Hey, Sadie, don't you think you had enough?" Sam said kindly.

Sadie did not appreciate Sam getting in her business, "Sam, you do the pouring and I do the drinking."

Sam chuckled, "Okay, anything you say, pretty lady. You know I got this gut feeling that you really don't belong in a place like this".

Sadie picked up her drink and took a sip, "Well, Sam how do you know that? Are you psychic??

"No, I'm not, but I know girls like you," Sam said.

Sadie replied, "And what kind of girl is that?"

Sam started to wipe the counter then stopped and looked at Sadie, "Church girls."

Sadie rolled her eyes, "Oh no, not you too. I am not a church girl!! I am a woman that has everything I need. and my man Eddie takes good care of me."

"Yeah, sure he does, that's why he's over there talking to another woman," Sam said as he nodded his head in Eddie's direction.

"Awe, Sam, it's just business that's all," Sadie said but her faced showed she didn't really believe the words she was saying.

Sam smiled, "Okay it's business if you say so. Look Sadie, you take care of yourself, okay. I know dudes like Eddie, and it always turns out for the worst".

Sadie patted Sam on the shoulder, "Sam, thank you but I've had one daddy already and I don't need another one. Besides, I am his main woman. He takes me home every night not them." Sadie finished the rest of her drink and stood up, "Well, time for me to get back on stage".

Sam took her empty glass and winked at her, "Take it easy, Sadie".

Sadie was back on stage singing her next set., Eddie walked over to Sam.

Eddie sat at the bar and motioned for Sam to come over to him, "Hey, I saw you talking to my woman!!" Sam shook his head, "Yeah, man, just small talk."

"Well, you keep it that way, Sam. I would hate for you to lose your job," Eddie threatened.

"Eddie, man, you don't need to threaten me. We were just talking," Sam said clearly upset.

"Just remember, you don't want to mess with old Eddie!!!"

Sam knew there was no reasoning with Eddie when he was like this, "Alright man, you know we are boys."

"Let's keep it that way. Don't touch my property!!! This is a good investment for me, and I don't want anybody to mess that up, you got that?" Eddie asked.

Sam, "Yeah, it's cool."

After the show, Eddie told one of his boys to take Sadie home because he had something to do.

Sadie protested, "Eddie, why can't I go with you? You know we never spend time together anymore."

"Look woman," Eddie said, "I told you I had something to do!!!"

Sadie kept persisting, "Eddie, you leave me at home every night!!! I want you to come home with me!!! Please, Eddie, I'm lonely at home." Eddie pulled Sadie close to him and Sadie thought her persistence had paid off but then he slapped her across the face.

Eddie clenched his jaw, "I told you, woman, I got business to take care of. Now, do what I say and go home." Sadie ran out the club crying and got into a cab. When Sadie got home she started drinking. Eddie's boy Roscoe was there at the house with her.

Roscoe said, "Sadie, I'm not trying to get into your business, but you really need to stop drinking so much." Roscoe seemed sincere but Sadie did not care.

Sadie looked Roscoe in the eyes, "Well you know what? You are getting into my business, and you need to leave." Sadie got another drink and fell on the floor crying.

Roscoe knelt and brushed Sadie's hair out of her eyes, "Sadie, what's wrong?"

"Just go away and leave me alone." Sadie yelled.

Roscoe stayed where he was, "Hey, I can't leave you like this!!"

Sadie sobbed, "You might as well, no one cares about me!!!"

"Don't say that. Eddie cares, but it is in a different way," Roscoe said

Sadie continued crying, "Whatever!!" Roscoe tried to pick Sadie up off the floor and they began to kiss. The kissing was intense, and Sadie didn't want it to stop.

Roscoe pulled away, "Sadie, this is wrong. We shouldn't do this. Eddie is my boy, and this is wrong."

Sadie touched Roscoe's faced, "What Eddie don't know won't hurt him. Roscoe, I am lonely, and I just need someone to hold me." Sadie and Roscoe kissed again but with more passion. Roscoe picked Sadie up and took her to the bedroom.

Later, Roscoe was nervous and scared. "I can't believe that happened!! Look, Sadie, please don't..."

Sadie sighed, "Roscoe don't worry. I won't tell Eddie".

Roscoe was still nervous, "Look, I have to go now."

"Yeah, you should go before you get in trouble with your boss," Sadie said sarcastically.

Roscoe scoffed, "Sadie, it's not like that!! Eddie is my boy, and he would kill me if he knew we were together."

"Like I said, you don't have to worry, he will never find out," Sadie said.

Roscoe put on his coat and headed towards the door, "Are you sure you are going to be okay?"

"I'll be fine, Roscoe. Good night," Sadie said. As soon as Roscoe left, Sadie started to cry again as she realized that she was losing herself. "Oh God, what am I doing? This is not the type of life that I want to live!! I have to do something about this before I die!!!" Sadie cried herself to sleep.

Eddie finally got home around five o clock in the morning. He walked into the living room and turned on the television. He noticed that he left the video camera on from a previous video shoot, and he started to watch the video. Eddie was in for the shock of his life. The tape showed Sadie and Roscoe kissing. "What the hell is this?" Eddie said out loud. "That dude was in my house with my woman!!! I am going to kill him and Sadie too". Eddie was so furious he started screaming and shouting. Eddie went into the bedroom and started screaming at Sadie.

"Sadie, wake up!! What the hell is going on here!! You messing with my boys now!! Girl, you have lost your mind!!!" Eddie screamed.

Sadie was shocked, "Eddie, Eddie, wait, Roscoe approached me!!! I told him to stop but..." Sadie had no idea there was a video that Eddie had seen.

"It didn't look like you told him to stop to me!!!" Eddie shouted.

Sadie realized what had happened, "Oh my god, you had the video on!!!"

"You're darn right and I saw everything! You need to get out of my house!" Eddie said matter of fact.

Sadie begged, "Eddie, wait a minute you need to hear my side of the story."

"I don't need to hear your side of the story. I saw everything I needed to see... now get out!" Eddie grabbed Sadie and pushed her towards the door.

"Eddie, I have no place to go," Sadie cried.

"Well, you should have thought about that before you sleptwith my friend," Eddie responded. Sadie pulled on Eddie's arm, "Eddie, please don't put me out. I will do anything for you."

"Anything?" Eddie question.

Sadie pleaded, "Yes, anything. I don't have anyone else."

Eddie contemplated, "Okay I tell you what. I want you to keep working at the night club and also, I have some customers… friends I mean, that like to have a good time when the club closes."

Sadie was unsure what he was asking, "What do you mean, Eddie?"

"You know what I mean!" Eddie shot back. "Now you know you need a place to stay so that is how you will repay me since you don't pay any bills around here. Now what do you say?"

"All right, Eddie, anything you say," Sadie agreed.

Eddie touched her chin, "Now share some of that love with old Eddie." Sadie was crying and so scared because she knew that she has gotten herself into some trouble,

Chapter 10

Six months later things had gone from bad to worse. Sadie was expecting. She was still working at the restaurant and Eddie was pimping women on the street and selling drugs. Sadie was working hard, and Jerome was happy to still have her. He genuinely wanted to make sure she was okay.

Jerome watched Sadie put away some cups, "Girl, how long do you think you can keep working on your feet? You're working for me in the daytime, and at the club at night... you know that baby is really growing."

Sadie smiled, "OhIi know. Did I tell you I am having a boy? I am going to name him Eddie Jr." Sadie rubbed her belly, . "Mr. Gray, can I tell you something? I really love Eddie. I know we need to get married. He says we are going to get married after the baby is born. We are planning a big wedding."

Jerome was listening intently to what Sadie was saying. When she finished, he said, "Sadie, there is something that I need to tell you." As he was about to speak some customers walked in. "I will tell you later," he said.

At the end of her shift, Sadie was sitting down rubbing her feet and counting her tips. Jerome walked in.

.

"Hey, let me rub your feet," Jerome said.

Sadie was hesitant, “Oh, that’s okay, Mr. Gray.”

Jerome persisted, “Let me rub your feet. you need a break, Sadie”. Jerome started rubbing Sadie’s feet just as Eddie walked in.

“Hey, what’s going on in here?” Eddie demanded.

Sadie tried to diffuse Eddie, “Oh, Eddie he was just...”

Eddie walked aggressively towards them, “I know what he was doing. Get your hand off my woman.”

Jerome stood his ground, “Look, man, don’t come in here talking loud like you going to do something. We can take this outside.”

Eddie accepted the challenge, “Well let’s take it outside then”

“Hey, Hey, ya’ll stop it, just stop it. Nothing is going on, Eddie. He was just trying to help me out,” Sadie explained.

Eddie responded but did not take his eyes off Jerome, “Sadie, go and get in the car. Now!” Eddie walked toward Jerome, “Look, you don’t know who you are messing with. I will cut your throat.” Eddie pulled out his knife. “Sadie is my property!! Do I make myself clear? I am her daddy now and you need to back off.”

Eddie didn’t scare Jerome, “Man I know your type. Too bad Sadie don’t know.” Eddie put his knife away and slammed the door.

Eddie and Sadie drove in silence. Sadie knew she was in for it when they got to the apartment. As soon as they got inside Eddie started, “Look, girl, let me get something straight with you. You are my woman. You just don’t get it do you? I own you. You are my property. You got that?”

Sadie didn't like when he called her property. She wanted to stand up to him, "Eddie, I am not your property, and you don't own me." Eddie reached for Sadie and knocked her down to the ground. She landed forcefully on her stomach.

"Yeah, that's what I thought. You do what I say or find another place to stay," Eddie said. Sadie started to cry. She was confused and angry and in physical pain from being knocked to the ground. She didn't know what to do. Eddie's phone rang. It was one of his boys and they needed him. Without a word, Eddie walked out the door and left Sadie lying there on the floor. Sadie stayed there for a while trying to figure out what to do. When she tried to get up, she started experiencing severe stomach pain. Sadie picked up the phone to call her friend Sissy. Sissy answered and Sadie could tell she was drunk and high. She was with Foster again and that was never a good thing.

"Sissy, I need some help. I am having severe pain and I think something is wrong with the baby," Sadie explained. Foster grabbed the phone out of Sissy's hand, told Sadie to take care of her own problems, and hung up.

Sadie started crying even harder. The pain was getting worse. and she fell back on the floor. "God please help me, somebody help me," Sadie screamed. At that moment, Eddie's friend walked through the door. He found Sadie on the floor, screaming for help.

"What happened?" Eddie's friend asked.

"Call 911. I think I am losing my baby," Sadie cried.

"Okay, don't worry everything will be okay. I will call Eddie."

"No, no don't call Eddie. Just get me to the hospital," Sadie pleaded. He called 911 and the ambulance came to take Sadie to the hospital. Sadie arrived at the hospital and the doctor examined her. He explained that Sadie was hemorrhaging and needed emergency surgery. The doctor asked for her husband or relative so that they could give permission for the surgery since Sadie could not respond. Eddie's friend was frightened at this point and began pacing the floor. He told the doctor he was just a friend of the baby's father but to do what needed to be done. He called Eddie but he did not answer his phone. He drove to the club where Eddie usually hung out and did his business and he was there.

"Sadie is in the hospital getting prepped for an emergency c-section and the baby might die. . "You need to go now," Eddie's friend explained with urgency.

Eddie responded, "Man, I am not going there. I am busy handling my business."

"Whatever, man, I got to go," Eddie's friend left the club. Even he couldn't believe how cold-hearted Eddie was being.

Chapter 11

Sadie was fighting for her life in emergency surgery and the doctors were doing everything they could do, but it was too late. The baby died and Sadie was in critical condition. She was transferred to the ICU. Sissy walked into the ICU unit, stumbling, her hair all over the place, she was drunk, and a total mess. Sissy approached a nurse, "I am looking for Sadie Ward."

"Are you a relative?" the nurse asked.

Sissy slurred her answer, "No, no, no. She is my best friend and I need to see her now. I think she is dying."

"We can only let relatives visit. It is against hospital policy to let non-relatives visit. I'm sorry," the nurse explained.

"Ma'am please, please, let me see my friend. I have to see her tonight. She is dying," Sissy sobbed.. The nurse had compassion and let Sissy visit for a few minutes. Sissy walked into the room and fell down on her knees crying when she saw Sadie.

"Oh my god, what happened, Sadie? What happened!!!" Sissy sobbed. Sadie tried to open her eyes when she heard Sissy's voice. Sissy walked over to Sadie's bed. Sadie opened her eyes, "Sissy, is that you? Sissy, I lost my baby, my baby is dead. I am so hurt right now," Sadie reached out for Sissy's hand.

Sissy tried to soothe Sadie, "Don't cry, Sadie everything is going to be all right." Sissy began to sing, "As long as you keep your head to the sky, you can win." When she finished singing the song, she brushed the hair off Sadie's forehead and said,. "Sadie, I am here for you. I am not going anywhere. I am here for you. Listen, Sadie I have seen better days, but I will be all right. We are both going through it, you know? But we are going to make it. I just got caught up with the wrong guy and started doing bad things, but I know better. I'm going to get my life together and you are too."

The doctor came to the room to check on Sadie He told her they tried everything they could to save the baby. He told her that she would need to stay for a couple of days before going home. Once the doctor left the room Sadie questioned Sissy, "What is really going on with you, girl? You know you can talk to me."

Sissy put her off, "We don't need to talk about me right now. We just need to make sure that you get well, so you can get out of here. I am thinking about going to rehab for about a couple of months to get myself together and you know what, when you get out we are going to get back together and hang out again."

Sadie took Sissy's hand, "I wish I was able to help you, but I am going through so much right now with Eddie. He is so jealous and crazy. I have to get away from him before he tries to kill me. I am so afraid of him,"

Sissy shook her head, "You better get away from him before someone gets hurt. You don't have to take that." Sissy stood up and squeezed Sadie's hand, "I have to go now, okay? Take care of yourself and don't forget to pray. I will miss you. I love you.". Sissy walked out of the room. As she entered the hallway to get on the elevator, she spotted Eddie coming down the hallway. Sissy immediately went the other way. A nurse stopped Eddie as he was entering the ICU.

"Can I help you, sir?" the nurse asked.

Eddie responded, "Yeah, I am looking for Sadie."

"What is Sadie's last name?" the nurse asked.

Eddie stuttered. He didn't know her last name, "Uh, uh..."

The nurse replied, "Sadie Ward? Are you a relative?"

"Yeah, I'm her uh husband," Eddie lied.

The nurse showed Eddie the room and he opened the door and walked in.

Eddie sat in the chair next to Sadie's bed, "Hey, hey, Sadie girl. What are you trying to do to my reputation by being in this here hospital? Are you trying to make me look bad? I don't have time for this. You are making me lose a lot of money running around looking for you".

Sadie tried to stay calm. She nervously said, "I am getting ready to call security. I want you to leave me alone and get out of here."

Eddie got close to Sadie's face, "Don't make me hurt you again because I will. I don't care about you being in this hospital or calling security. Let me tell you something, I have invested a lot of money in you, and I own you now. You are my property, you understand? You are mine, and you will do what I tell you to do. You got that!!!" Eddie rubbed Sadie's face, "Now, baby girl, you just get your pretty self together and I will be back in a couple of days to pick you up. You have wasted a lot of money in here and now you owe Eddie. Get your rest and I will be back in two days to pick up my property." Eddie walked out of the room laughing. Sadie started crying and calling for the nurse. She asked for a sleeping pill. She just needed to rest.

Chapter 12

Sadie fell asleep quickly after taking the medicine and began to dream about when she was a little girl sitting in church with her parents. She dreamed about singing in the youth choir and leading the song "His Eye is on the Sparrow." She saw the congregation all standing up and giving her a standing ovation. Then her dream took her to a place in her life where she became a famous gospel artist. She was singing at the Apollo in New York and her parents were in the audience waiting for the concert to start. In her dream, Sadie walked on the stage and began to thank her parents for believing in her. After she thanked her parents, she also thanked her best friend Sissy who was in the audience as well. Suddenly, Eddie appeared. He was trying to discourage her and tear her down. She turned to her right and saw that Eddie had a gun in his hand. He pulled the trigger and shot Sadie. The people in the theater started running and screaming. Sadie fell to the floor with a bullet wound to her chest. Her parents tried to go to her rescue, but it was too late.

Sadie woke up from her dream screaming causing the nurse to run into the room. Sadie let the nurse know it was just a bad dream. Sadie couldn't shake the feeling that this dream was a warning. She had to get away from Eddie. She was sure of that now. She was able to fall back asleep and sleep until the next morning. Sadie was resting the next day when Jerome walked into the room. He had a black eye and a large bandage on his chin

Jerome knocked on the door and then went in, "Well, how is the patient?"

Sadie was surprised to see him, "I am doing better. How did you find out that I was here?"

"You know how it is!! Word gets around fast in a small neighborhood," Jerome answered.

Sadie could not ignore the black eye, "What happened to your face?"

Jerome touched his black eye, "Oh it's nothing to worry about. I will be fine. That's not what is important now anyways. How are you really doing? I am sorry about the baby."

Sadie's eyes filled with tears, "I've seen better days, but God has been good to me. So, I can't complain."

Jerome pulled out flowers from behind his back, "These are for you."

Sadie was shocked, "Thank you so much. They are beautiful."

Jerome smiled, "You are welcome, beautiful lady."

Sadie smoothed her hair down, "Well, I don't think I look so beautiful now. I have not had a chance to comb my hair or put on my makeup."

Jerome replied, "Sadie, you are beautiful without makeup. How long are you going to be cooped up in this dreadful place?"

Sadie set the flowers on the table next to the bed, "The doctor said I could go home tomorrow. How is the restaurant coming along without me?"

"We are trying to manage. You know it is not the same without you, but I don't want you to worry about a thing. Take all the time you need to get well. I am going to pay you for sick time for two weeks so you can get back on your feet.".

Sadie couldn't believe how kind he was being, "Thank you, Mr. Gray, you have been so generous.

Jerome chuckled, "Hey, I told you to call me Jerome".

Sadie smiled, "Well, Jerome, thank you."

Jerome took Sadie's hand, "I am here for you whatever you need. You have my cell phone number. You can call me anytime. Now get some rest." Jerome kissed Sadie on the cheek and walked out of the room.

When Jerome got to the elevator, Eddie was there. They both looked at each other with anger in their eyes. They began to walk around each other.

Eddie couldn't let it go, "Man, you just don't get enough do you. You keep showing up like a bad dream and you just don't get the picture. Looks like old Eddie got to take drastic measures now." Eddie pointed his fingers like a gun in Jerome's face. "I told you to stay away from my property!! I own Sadie, How many times do I have to keep reminding you of that!!! Are you slow, man?"

Jerome laughed, "Look man, you don't scare me with all that crazy talk. Anyway, talk is cheap. If you want to do something, let's take it outside, again. Looks like I got the best of you. Look at you. All I got was this black eye." Eddie had a cast on his arm, a bandage on his nose, and was walking with a cane because he had a bruised knee. Jerome started laughing while walking away.

Eddie called after him, "Hey man, you really don't want to mess with me. Don't let this face fool you. You dig!!! Don't make me call my boys, because I will."

Jerome looked over his shoulder, "Call your boys!! They will get whipped just like you did." Eddie turned around and made a shooter sign at Jerome. Then he walked away laughing. "Yeah, you better watch your back," Eddie mumbled to himself.

Eddie went to Sadie's room and found her sleeping. He started talking to her while she slept. "Yeah, baby, you go ahead and get your sleep now. Don't worry about a thing. Old Eddie will take care of everything. Just like I told you before, you are my property, and I own you."

Eddie left and started walking towards his car. His phone started to ring, "Yeah, this Eddie speak to me, baby. How much do you need? Meet me on Seventh and Sunset Street around nine. I will be there man, just have my money."

Chapter 13

Sadie woke up when she heard the door close. She realized that someone had been in her room. Sadie stretched but had a weird sensation, "Oh my god, I can't feel my legs. Sadie started screaming and frantically pushed the button to call for a nurse

When the nurse came to the room Sadie shouted, "I can't feel my legs!! Am I paralyzed? I can't move my legs." The nurse went to call the doctor. Sadie was frantic and scared, but she remembered to pray, "Oh Lord, God please help me. I need you now, Father, to come to my rescue. Father, please hear my prayer, oh Lord, and attend unto my groaning. In Jesus name I pray. Amen." The doctor came to the room, "I'm Dr. Rider. Let me just examine you before we panic."

Dr. Rider examined Sadie by pricking her toes and her legs. Sadie did not feel anything. Dr. Rider ordered several test including an MRI. Sadie looked at Dr. Rider and said, "I will be able to walk again. I know that this is only a test of my faith and I believe God is going to heal me. We have to believe in a higher power. It is all in God's hands."

Dr. Rider and the nurse left the room in order to start working on Sadie's case immediately. Sadie was left all alone and started praying again silently. While she was praying, a woman walked into her room with a long white dress. She was very beautiful and radiant. Sadie stared at her as she walked into the room.

"May I help you?" Sadie asked.

"Oh, I'm sorry, I am looking for a friend of mine," the mysterious woman said.

"I think you are in the wrong room," Sadie said.

"My friend told me she was in room 111. She was having some problems with her legs and was admitted to the hospital. I just came by to pray with her and let her know that God hears her prayers and sees her tears. I wanted to let her know that all she needs to do is put her trust in the Lord and she will receive her healing. I am sorry to bother you," she explained.

Sadie's phone rang and as she reached for the phone she said, "Wait. What is your name?" but when she turned around the woman had already left the room. The phone stopped ringing.

"That was so strange!!!" Sadie thought to herself, "Maybe she was an angel. God, if she was an angel, thank you."

Dr. Rider walks into the room with a technician to take Sadie for her tests. In spite of everything, Sadie smiled, "Don't worry, Dr. Rider. Everything will be okay." The medical tech started rolling Sadie to x-ray when they ran into Eddie who was on his way to Sadie's room.

"Hey, where are you taking her? Where are you going?" Eddie asked.

I have to go to x-ray for some tests. I may be paralyzed," Sadie explained.

"Paralyzed!!! That is impossible!! This cannot be happening to me. I mean to you!!! How did this happen? I was here yesterday, and the doctor said you were okay, and you were going home today. What happened? Do you realize that she is my responsibility? I demand to know where you are taking her and why!!!" Eddie shouted.

"Sir, Sadie is experiencing some paralysis and we need to take her to x-ray," the technician replied.

"Just go to the waiting room and we will let you know something as soon as we can."

Eddie grabbed Sadie's hand, "Sadie I will be waiting for you!

Sadie pulled her hand away, "I want you to leave this hospital now, and I never want to see you again."

Eddie chuckled, "You must be on some kind of medication. I will see you later." .

About an hour after the tests, Dr. Rider went to Sadie's room with the results.

"Sadie, I'm very sorry but the x-rays and MRI show that you are permanently paralyzed."

Sadie begins to cry, "Oh my Lord, I can't believe it!!! What am I going to do now? How will I get around? I cannot work in this condition."

Dr. Rider pats Sadie on the hand, "I am so sorry. We will make arrangements for rehab."

"I need to be alone right now. I need to process this," Sadie said through her tears.

Once she was alone, Sadie began to talk to the Lord, "Now, Lord, I am asking you to hear my prayer. Oh Lord, attend unto my groaning and my mourning. Lord I need a miracle to happen right now in your name. You know, Lord. I have not forgotten the messages that I heard as a little girl about faith. How if we only have faith the size of a mustard seed, we can move mountains. Well, God, I am working my faith right now. Just give me the strength to make it through. In the name of Jesus, I pray. Amen"

Just as Sadie said Amen, Eddie walked into the room and fell down on his knees.

"Yes, Lord, we need you to do this for us. Yes, Yes, Amen!!" Eddie prayed.

"What are you doing in my room? How did you get in here? Visiting hours are over and I told you not to come back. Security! Security! Somebody help," Sadie yelled

"Shut-up before I have to…" Eddie raised his hand to hit her.

"Say it!! Before you hit me? Go ahead, Eddie, hit me and I will scream so loud the police will hear me from miles away. Now get out of my room before I call security again," Sadie yelled.

Eddie lowered his hand, "All right, Sadie, you want to play that game? That is cool with me. Just remember, you belong to me, don't forget it." As Eddie left the room, he turned around quickly and gave Sadie the shooter sign and started laughing.

Eddie left the hospital and got in the car with his lady friend who was waiting for him.

"It's cold out here. What took you so long? Was your mother okay?" the girl asked.

Eddie grabbed her arm, "Shut up, Denise, I'm in charge, you got that!!! I am the boss, when I say wait you do just that!"

Denise was trembling, "Okay, Eddie. I'm sorry baby. I was just cold and... "

"I don't care about that!!! I was taking care of my business and you need to wait," Eddie shot back.

Chapter 14

The next day Sadie woke up feeling great and thanking the Lord for a brand new day.

Sadie knew that God heard her prayer last night and she decided she was going to walk by faith and not by sight.

Dr. Rider came into the room, "Good morning, Sadie. How are you feeling today?"

Sadie smiled, "I'm on top of the world. Nothing can ruin my day. I prayed and I know that God is going to heal me. I have faith."

Dr. Rider returns her smile, "That is good! I want you to keep that same attitude. I am going to do everything possible in order for you to walk again. I also believe in a higher power, and we are going to make it through this." They shook hands and smiled at each other. Dr. Rider leaned close to Sadie and all at once kissed her.

Sadie started screaming, "Oh my god!!! You are a pervert!!! Get out of here!!! Help, somebody help me!!!You are a quack for a doctor, and I want you fired immediately." Sadie reached for the call button to call the nurse. She kept pushing the button, but didn't realize that she was pushing the button that turned the volume up for the television. The louder she yelled, the louder the television got.

Dr. Rider headed to the door, "Sadie please calm down. I am leaving… I'm sorry, I don't know what happened!!"

"This cannot be happening to me," Sadie says out loud. She picks up the phone to call Aunt Neisse.

"Aunt Neisse? This is Sadie. I need you to come and pick me up from the hospital. They are releasing me today."

"Let me see if I can get me a ride up there," Aunt Neisse responded.

"Where is your car?" Sadie asked.

Aunt Neisse sighed, "I sold that car last week. I needed some groceries. You know how it is. I will figure it out though. You just wait right there. Old Aunt Neisse won't let you down." Sadie started crying. What was happening to her? How many tragedies could one girl handle.

Jerome came into the room with more flowers, "Hello, sunshine! How's the most beautiful girl in the world doing?"

"Honestly, terrible. Everything I thought could go wrong has. I got to get out of this hospital today, right now this minute," Sadie explained.

"You're being discharged today?" Jerome asked.

"Well, uh, something like that. We don't need to talk about that right now… How are you doing? Your face looks much better," Sadie said.

Jerome laughed, "That's what home remedies can do for you. Do you have a ride home?"

"Yeah, my Aunt Neisse is coming to pick me up around 10:00. She said she was going to get a ride," Sadie explained.

"Let me take you home. You know how your aunt is. You will be waiting on her until the next morning," Jerome said.

"Jerome, I just experienced something that was so terrible!! I am so embarrassed!!! Promise me if I tell you, you won't 'tell anyone," Sadie asked.

Jerome looked concerned, "You got my word. What happened?"

"The doctor was in my room this morning and he, he kissed me!! Oh my god, he kissed me. My doctor!!" Sadie cried.

Jerome could not believe it, "What!!! He did what!!! Did you report him?"

"Not yet, I was in a state of shock I didn't know what to do," Sadie explained. Jerome jumped up and began to walk out the door.

Sadie yelled after him, "Where are you going? Come back!!! You promised you wouldn't say anything!"

"Sadie, someone needs to know about this. I am going to find out who is over the hospital board," Jerome said.

"No, please don't say anything right now. I just want to go home and once I get settled; I will report it."

Jerome still looked concerned, "Are you able to walk now?"

"No, I am getting ready to start rehabilitation for one month, and then I pray to God that I will be able to walk again."

Jerome started gathering Sadie's things, "Well, let me help you pack your things, and I will take you home. If your aunt gets a ride, which I doubt very seriously, you don't know where you will end up. I will take you wherever you need to go." Jerome packed her things and then went to the nurse's station to get a wheelchair.

The attending doctor, Dr. Field walked into the room with Sadie's discharge papers to go to rehab. Dr. Field said, "Hello, Ms. Ward, I am Dr. Field, taking over for Dr. Rider. I just need you to sign these discharge papers and we will let you go home today."

Sadie signed the papers and started packing a few last things into her makeup case., Eddie walked into the room. "Hey, where do you think you going? I told you that I was coming to pick you up. Why didn't you call me?"

Sadie could not believe him, "Eddie, I don't need you to do nothing for me. It is over between you and me."

Eddie hit his fist into his hand, "Oh you think so? Girl, I told you that I own you. Don't make me act a fool in this hospital because I will. Now get your things and let's go.

"I said I'm not going anywhere with you," Sadie said determinedly.

Jerome walked into the room, "I got the wheel… man what are you doing in here? Didn't the lady tell you she didn't want to see you anymore!! You just don't get it, do you?"

"Man, shut up!! This is my business, and Sadie is my property," Eddie yelled.

"Your property? You don't have any respect for the lady. She is not a piece of meat!!!"

Sadie started crying and screaming, "Stop it! Stop it you two. I cannot take this anymore!"

Aunt Neisse walked into the room drunk and stumbling, "Sadie, Sadie, baby, auntie is here, baby, here for you. Let's go. I had to pay someone to come pick you up, now hurry. We can't keep the man waiting,"

Sadie was overwhelmed, "Aunt Neisse, please take me home now. I want to go home." Dr. Rider entered the room. He wanted to apologize before Sadie left.

Dr. Rider started, "Sadie, I just want to say that... uh what is going on in here? This patient needs her rest..."

Jerome started towards the doctor, "Yeah right, she needs rest, rest in your arms you mean? I should punch you in the face right now. What kind of doctor are you?"

"What? You been trying to talk to my woman? Now I know I'm going to kick you!!!" Eddie said.

"Sir, it was not like that, calm down and listen," Dr. Rider said.

Jerome got close to the doctor's face, "Hey man, you are supposed to be the professional here and now you going around kissing your patients. What kind of mess is that!!"

"Kissing patients!!! Man, you put your hands on my woman!!!" Eddie drew his fist back to hit Doctor Rider as security walked in.

The security officer said, "Hey, keep it down in here. Everybody has to get out now."

"Not me, I came to pick up Sadie," Aunt Sadie said.

"Nobody is going anywhere with my woman. She is going home with me," Eddie said.

"Sir is this your wife?" the security officer asked.

"No, but she is mine." Eddie answered. Sadie was so upset that she began to get nauseated and started vomiting. Everyone ran to Sadie to try to help

Aunt Neisse started stumbling towards the door, "Sadie, baby, you can't get in my man's car throwing up girl. He just got his car cleaned today and it is the bomb.”.

Dr. Rider yelled over the chaos, “Someone call the nurse.” The nurse rushed into the room to give Sadie a shot to make her feel better.

“Everybody get out now!!!! I mean now... I will call the police, if you don’t. We have to take care of our patient. Enough of the drama. Take it outside,” the nurse said. .Everyone left the room including Dr. Rider. The nurse got Sadie comfortable and fifteen minutes later Sadie was asleep.

Chapter 15

Eddie, Jerome, and Aunt Neisse were all outside the hospital yelling and screaming at each other.

"Hey, you all are the reason why Sadie got sick!!" Eddie yelled.

Jerome yells back, "Man what do you mean? If it weren't for you, Sadie would not be in this hospital in the first place."

"Whatever, you don't know what you are talking about. I will take Sadie home when she is better," Eddie replied.

"Man, Sadie isn't going nowhere with you. She told me that she wanted me to take her home," Jerome shot back.

"Oh, she did!!! Well, I will see about that. I am tired of that little..." Eddie responded.

Jerome wasn't finished, "Why do you think she wants to be with someone like you? You are so disrespectful!! Just leave her alone."

Eddie's jaw is clenched in anger, "That's it man!!! I can't take it anymore". Eddie pulled out his gun and pointed it at Jerome. Dr. Rider walked outside. As he approached them, the gun went off. Dr. Rider fell to the ground. Eddie, Jerome, and Aunt Neisse all stood in disbelief. Eddie thought about running away but the police, security, and the other hospital staff ran outside to see what happen. It was too late for him to try and get away. Dr. Rider was lying there on the ground with a gunshot wound to the chest. There was an uproar outside as everyone was trying to find out what happened. One of the hospital staff brought out a stretcher and they transported Dr. Rider to emergency surgery. The police had Eddie in custody. He was in a police car while they sorted everything out. The police were questioning Jerome and wanted him to go down to the police station. Jerome got into the other squad car and they took them both downtown.

In the emergency room Dr. Rider was fighting for his life. Dr. Field walked into the waiting room to let everyone know the status of Dr. Rider's condition. Dr. Rider's wife, Bertha and his kids were there.

Dr. Field said, "Bertha, Stan is going to be fine. He will be in ICU for a couple of days so we can monitor him. The surgery was serious, but we were able to remove the bullet."

"Thank you, Ben, thank you for everything. Can we see him now?' Mrs. Rider asked.

He is resting right now. You and the children need to go home and get some rest and come back in the morning. He is on a lot of medication and is heavily sedated. Just go home, Bertha and get some rest, Trust me,"

Dr. Field walked into Sadie's room to check on Sadie. Sadie was sound asleep. Sadie heard the door close and woke up. Sadie felt dizzy and confused. She wasn't sure what was going on. The last thing she remembered was everyone was in her room and someone was coming to pick her up to go home. Sadie didn't want to sleep anymore so she turned on the TV. The news stated that there was a shooting at St. Laurel's hospital at 8:00 pm that night. Then the they flashed pictures of Eddie, Jerome, and Dr. Rider. Sadie panic and called for the nurse.

The nurse called over the intercom, "We will be there shortly, Ms. Ward."

As the nurse got ready to go to Sadie's room, another nurse stopped her. "Did you hear why Dr. Rider got shot?"

"No, I thought the police were still investigating," said Sadie's nurse.

"Her and Dr. Rider had a thing going on and that is why he got shot, her boyfriend shot Dr. Rider because he caught them together. I wonder if she knew that he was married, and his wife is pregnant?"

"Well, let me go and see what she needs," Sadie's nurse replied. The nurse walked into Sadie's room, "What can I do for you, Ms. Ward?"

Sadie asked, "Was there a shooting tonight at the hospital? Is Dr. Rider okay?"

"Yes, there was a shooting, but everything is under control now. He had surgery and is now in ICU ,. I am sure everything will be okay. Do you need anything?" the nurse asked.

"No, thank you," Sadie replied. When she got back to the nurse's station, the other nurses wanted to know what Sadie said.

Sadie's nurse said, "She had the nerve to ask me about Dr.Rider, She wanted to know how her man was doing. She ought to be ashamed of herself," the nurse explained.

The next morning, the nurse's aide brought Sadie breakfast, "Did you sleep well?"

"Not really. I just have a lot on my mind, which makes it difficult to sleep," Sadie said.

"Do you want to talk about it?" the nurse's aide asked, "I got all day. I don't get off until 8:00 pm tonight. I'm all ears."

Sadie smiled, "Well, first of all, I am ready to go home. I was discharge from the hospital yesterday, but I didn't have a ride. Second, I feel like I have caused so much trouble around here that I just want to start all over again with my life."

"What you are asking for is not hard to accomplish at all. I can give you a ride home, that is not a problem. I have a break at ten and I can take you then. Secondly, you can start over again, just pray and God will take care of the rest," she said.

Sadie was in awe, "Thank you so much. I will be ready. Hey, what is your name?" Sadie asked.

"Peggy Barkley," she said.

Chapter 16

Down at the precinct, Eddie and Jerome were in the same cell. Eddie was under a $50,000 bond. Jerome was going to be released. Eddie was talking loud and yelling at the guard.

"Hey man, let me out of here!!! This is some bull!!! I don't belong in here. I got on a three- hundred-dollar suit and two-hundred-dollar alligator shoes and it's filthy in this place. Hey, y'all must not know who I am!! Man, let me make my phone call. I got a right to make a phone call!!" Eddie yelled.

"Hey, shut up!!! You need to shut your mouth!! You aren't making any call right now. What you need to do is shut up and calm down before I come in there and...," the guard yelled back.

"And what man! Are you threatening me man? Hey, did you hear that!! I need to call my lawyer. He will take care of all this mess. I got to get out of here and take care of some business. I am a businessman, and I am wasting time in this trashy place. I want my lawyer!!!" Eddie demanded

"Yeah, you are going to see your lawyer all right, after you spend the night here. So, you might as well calm down and put on this orange suit," the guard said. The guard started laughing and gave Eddie an orange suit.

"Man, I am not putting on that suit!!" Eddie yelled.

"Well, suit yourself!! Awe, man did you hear that? Just suit yourself... now that is funny!! I think I am in the wrong field. I should have been a comedian…you either put on the orange suite, or your birthday suit. Now what will it be?" the guard asked.

Eddie snatched the suit out of the jailer's hand. "Oh and by the way, Jerome Gray you are free to go," said the guard. Jerome walked towards the lobby. He saw his sister Jan.

"Hey little sis, thank you. I promise I will pay you back," Jerome said, hugging his sister.

"Whenever you get it, Jerome. I was so worried about you. What happened ? It was all on the news!!" Jan said.

"I'll tell you all about it later," said Jerome.

Chapter 17

Peggy pulled up the car and helped Sadie get in. She asked Sadie for directions to her house. Peggy didn't know that Sadie didn't have a home to go to. Sadie had to think of something to say.

"I left my key, and I can't get into the house. Let me call my roommate," Sadie said.

Sadie dialed Jerome's number and prayed someone would answer.

"Hello, hi, this is Sadie,"

"Are you okay?" Jerome asked.

Sadie had to find a way to let him know she was pretending he was her roommate. "Yes, I am great. I was wondering if you had the key to get into the house. I just wanted to make sure that you were at home because I was discharge from the hospital and I don't have my key. A friend of mind, Peggy is giving me a ride home," Sadie said.

"Oh, oh, I get it now. Sure, I will be home. My place is your place. and you are always welcome," Jerome said. They arrived at Jerome's house where Jerome and his sister Jan were waiting outside. Jerome walked over to the car and helped Sadie get out of the car into the wheelchair.

Sadie said goodbye to Peggy and thanked her for her help. .

"Sadie, this is my sister Jan," said Jerome.

"Nice to meet you, Jan," Sadie replied.

Sadie got settled into Jerome's house and they were resting in the living room

"Jerome, what happened last night? I saw everything on the new," Sadie asked.

"It was a disaster. Eddie is in a lot of trouble. He is under a $50,000 bond They took me down for questioning, but I was released tonight. We got into a confrontation outside of the hospital, and the next thing that I saw was Dr. Rider on the ground bleeding. I can't believe Eddie shot him. It was bad." Jerome explained.

"Oh my god!!! So, Eddie is probably going to prison," Sadie said.

"Yeah, I believe he is in big trouble this time. You know, out of all the trouble I've had with Eddie, my heart really goes out to him now. We are talking about murder!!" Jerome said.

"This is awful. I know I am going to have to appear in court and I really don't want to have anything to do with that. Oh. Jerome. I feel like all of this is my fault. I wish I hadn't got involved with Eddie from the beginning. If Dr. Rider dies, I just don't know what I will do," Sadie said.

While Jerome and Sadie were talking, there was a news flash regarding the shooting on television. The news reporter stated that there was a shooting at the hospital and one of the physicians was shot in the chest. The newscaster said that Dr. Rider was in stable condition, and they were able to remove the bullet successfully.

"Oh my goodness, that is a miracle!!! God must have heard my prayer," Sadie said.

"Yeah, you got that right Sadie. It had to be an act of God in order to save his life. Man, I was right there, and I saw him on the ground in a pool of blood. It was terrible," Jerome said.

"The good thing is that he is going to be all right. We should be thanking the Lord for the miracle that he has done," Sadie said.

"You know there has been so much going on the last couple of hours I forgot to ask you about yourself. How did you get out of the hospital so soon?" Jerome asked.

"It doesn't matter, I am out now, and I start rehab on Monday morning at the restoration facility. Jerome, I have been through so much that I just need to relax my mind and concentrate on walking again. I have prayed to God that I will be healed and will no longer need this wheelchair." Sadie said.

"I am going to help you in every way that I can to see to it that you will walk again. Right now, you and I need to get some rest until the morning, and we will start a fresh and brand new day. I am going to sleep on the couch, and you can have my room," Jerome said. Jerome lifted Sadie out of the chair and into the bed. As he does, he almost drops Sadie and they both start laughing.

"Sweet dreams, thank you Jerome," Sadie says gratefully.

Chapter 18

Eddie got the money together and was able to be released on bond.

"Yeah, I thought so. I told you man, nothing can hold old Eddie down and don't you forget, I am going to make sure that you get fired!!" Eddie yelled at the guards as he walked by. Eddie was escorted to the front office where he picked up his valuables and he discovered that his watch was missing.

"Hey, what a minute!! Which one of you stole my Rolex? Now I know I have to press charges against the entire county. I know one of you stole my watch! It cost me five thousand grand, and somebody better cough it up now!!" Eddie shouted.

The guard explained that Eddie only came in with a gold bracelet, two diamond rings, and a medallion. He did not have on a watch. Eddie argued with him to no avail.

"I better get out of here before somebody gets hurt. You will hear from my lawyer, and I am going to sue this whole precinct for stealing," Eddie shouted. Foster was out in the lobby waiting on Eddie.

Eddie got in Foster's face, "Hey, did you talk to my lawyer?"

"Yeah, I talked to your lawyer. Man, that dude is phony. You know he told me that he represented OJ Simpson, and he has never lost a case," Foster said.

Eddie smiled, "That's what I'm talking about man. He is the best lawyer in the state of New York."

"Eddie, you have to be kidding!! That guy is a phony and I know a crook when I see a crook because I'm a crook myself," Foster laughs.

"Well, I trust him, and I need a good lawyer right now. I know that I've gotten myself in a lot a trouble, but I believe my lawyer can get me out if I plead insanity," Eddie said with confidence. "Well, that doctor that you shot isn't dead. The news said that he is in stable condition," Foster explained.

"Oh man, that is good. For a moment there I thought I was going to be indicted for murder. You know what man? That is good news. Let's go get some grub and take me home," Eddie said.

"All right. You know your lady been crying and upset ever since you been locked up," Foster said.

"Fos, I don't care about that woman right now. Where is Sadie? Is she still in the hospital?" Eddie asked.

"I don't know where she is. If I were you, she would be the last thing on my mine right now. That's why you are in so much trouble now," Foster said.

"Hey, you think I don't know that!!! But that woman owes me big time, and it is time for her to pay up," Eddie said.

"You are asking for trouble. I knew the first time I saw her that she was trouble," Foster said.

"Shut up, man, you were running around the studio talking about how well she could sing!! You were thinking the same thing I was thinking...money," Eddie said.

"You know what, you got a point there. I was seeing dollars signs, but now I see trouble. You need to lay low right now until this entire situation is behind you," Foster said.

Eddie laughed, "You know old Eddie... what Eddie wants, Eddie gets. Now let's go so I can take care of business."

The next morning Eddie and Foster went down to the lawyer's office to take care of legal business. When they arrive, Eddie approached the receptionist, "Yeah, I need to speak to Mr. Ellington."

"Do you have an appointment?" the receptionist asked.

"No, I don't have an appointment, but I need to talk to him right now and I don't have time to waste with you. I am not coming back tomorrow. I need to see him today and I am not taking no for an answer!! Do you know who I am?" Eddie asked.

"No, I'm afraid I don't know who you are," the receptionist said.

"I am the Eddie Smith of New York. What do I have to do in order to see Mr. Ellington today?" Eddie asked. About that time Mr. Ellington heard all the commotion outside of his office and he came out to see what was going on. When Eddie saw him, he said, "What's up Roy, it's been a long time, man."

"Eddie. It sure has. Ms. Perry it's okay. I will see him today. We are long time buddies. Gentlemen, come to my office." Roy said.

"Look Roy, I need some help. I am quite sure you saw the news and I need a good lawyer to help me get out of this trouble. Now, I thought about just pleading insanity, I think that would…" Eddie tried to explain but Roy cut him off.

"Hold on, wait a minute!! I need you to calm down and relax. I need to get all the details before we make any decision," Roy said.

"What kind of details do you need, Roy? I know you saw the news, so you know what you need to do. Now a friend needs some help and I need it now. Is it money we're talking about? You know money has never been a problem. Whatever you need I will take care of you, as long as you take care of me. Besides, what are friends for? I watch your back and you watch mine. You know what I mean, Roy? I just can't forget what happened last year. If it weren't for me, you probably wouldn't be the great lawyer that you are. Right, Roy, I mean Mr. Ellington," Eddie said.

"Look, Eddie, that was the past. I don't live that type of life anymore," Roy explained.

"Yeah, it might be your past. but you know what they say, you can forgive but not forget. Now I need a favor. so I am looking for my friend to help me out!!" Eddie shouted.

"All right, Eddie. I will see what I can do," Roy promised.

"See what you can do? No man, you got it wrong!! You will take care of this for me!! I will be back tomorrow, and we will discuss this further." Before Eddie left, he picked up one of Roy's pictures of his wife and kids. "What a nice family, Roy. Man, you have the best of everything, a good job, a beautiful home, and beautiful family. Too bad Barbara chose you instead of me. I guess she wanted a fancy lawyer instead of a drug dealer. Yeah, that girl was fine," Eddie said with a sly smile.

Eddie, you are out of line, and I don't appreciate you talking that way about my wife," Roy said.

"Like I said, you owe me, and you need to help a friend out. I would hate to mess up that pretty little face," Eddie threatened.

"Hey, you all need to leave right now before I call security!!" Roy yelled.

"Okay man, calm down. I'll be back tomorrow at nine, don't be late," Eddie said as he waved goodbye. Eddie and Foster left Roy's office.

"Man, you are crazy!!! That is why I like hanging out with you. You always get what you want," Foster said shaking his head.

"That's right!! I am in charge now, Foster and nothing is going to stop me now. All I need to do now is get my hands on Sadie. She thinks that she has gotten away, but I have news for her. She owes me big time and it is time for her to pay," Eddie said.

"Eddie, I know you are in charge but maybe man; just maybe you need to leave well enough

alone. That girl has been through a lot in the last week and she needs to get herself together now. I heard she was paralyzed and confined to a wheelchair, and then on top of that she lost her baby." Foster explained.

"Hey man, that was my baby too!! How do you think I feel?" Eddie asked.

"Feel? Eddie, you don't have any feelings!! As long as you and I have been boys you have always thought about yourself and what you can get. You know how you do it man!!!" Foster said.

"Yeah, that's right!!! I know I'm not trying to get soft!! I got to check myself!!" Eddie laughed.

"That's right you better check yourself. I almost didn't know who you were for a minute there. Let's go and get some breakfast and then I got to go see how much money we made last night on the streets. Oh yeah, Eddie, I almost forgot!! Those girls said it was too cold to be out there last night." Foster said.

"What!! They have to remember we have the same motto as the mailman rain, sleet, snow or hail, we got to deliver!!!" Eddie joked.

Foster started laughing) After they ate, they went to straighten out those girls. They had money that Eddie needed, or he was going to rough some of them up. They stopped by the Midway Club on Fifth Street. When the pulled up to the club one of Eddie's girls was standing outside in the cold waiting for business to show up.

"Hey, Coco, are you having a problem tonight, girl?" Eddie asked.

"Oh, no, Eddie, no, I'm not having a problem!! Just waiting on a big spender to come by that's all," Coco said.

"So how long have you been out hear waiting on this big spender?" Eddie asked.

"Uh, well, uh..." Coco tried to come up with an answer.

"Yeah, that's what I thought... you don't have my money do you?" Eddie questioned.

"Well, Eddie, I just need a little more time." Coca said.

"Hey, you had all the time you needed now get in this car so I can punish you for not making old Eddie's money." Eddie threatened.

Coco begged for a change, "Eddie, please, please just give me another hour, I swear to you I will have your money."

"Look, Coco, it is too late. For one thing you are too old now. You know what I'm saying, Foster?" Eddie laughed.

"I need this job; I need to pay my bills man" Coco explained.

"If you don't get in this car, I will make sure that your girl Sadie will find out that you are working for me!" Eddie yelled.

"Ok Eddie, please don't tell Sadie." Coco responded.

"You drink too much, Coco. You can't do business for me when you are drunk all the time. Just get in the car I'm not gonna to say it again" Eddie grabbed her by the arm. Aunt Neisse aka Coco got into the car and Eddie drove off. She was in the back seat crying and scared of what might happen.

Chapter 19

Back at Jerome's house Sadie was waking up from a good night sleep. Jerome knocked on the door and told Sadie he was making some bacon, eggs, grits, and toast for breakfast. While Sadie was lying there waiting for breakfast, she started to feel some tingling in her feet and wiggling her toes. Sadie continued to move her toes and tried to see if she could get up on her own. Sadie managed to push herself up and swing her legs around to get out of the bed. She used all of her strength to lift herself up and tried to stand up.

"Ok God, I know that you are a miracle worker, and I know that I can do all things through Christ who gives me strength. Now Father, I am asking for your strength right now in the name of Jesus," Sadie prayed. When Sadie finished praying, she began to rise up her feet. "Oh my God, I can stand up!! Thank you, Jesus." Sadie began to take a step. She moved her right foot and then her left foot. "This is a miracle from God!!! Praise the Lord, glory to your name Father".

Jerome heard Sadie talking and ran quickly to make sure she was okay. "Sadie, are you alright? I heard you screaming. Do you need help?" Jerome asked concerned.

"Jerome, come in. Open the door!!" Sadie said excitedly. Jerome opened the door and found Sadie standing there on her feet.

"This is unbelievable!!! Look at you girl!! You are standing up" Jerome exclaimed.

"I know. It is a miracle from God!! Come over here and help me. I'm going to try to walk if I can." Sadie said with confidence. Sadie took her first step. "Look at me Jerome, I am walking again. God is awesome."

"Yes, He is. He is an awesome God," Jerome agreed.

The doorbell rang so Jerome told Sadie to wait there while he went to answer it. He opened the door and found Foster standing there.

"Man, what are you doing here, and how did you find out where I live? If you don't leave, I am going to call the police." Jerome threatened.

"Look, I just came to tell you to leave Sadie alone. Eddie is not the average man. He can be really dangerous, and I just want to let you know that you are playing with fire." Foster said.

"Man, look here. I am not scared of nobody you got that!! Now you need to get off my property before I call the police and have you arrested." Jerome yelled.

"All right, man, No need to call for drastic measures!! I just wanted to let you know that you need to watch your back." Foster said. Jerome slammed the door.

'Is everything ok? I heard the door slam." Sadie asked.

"Yeah, everything is okay, just a salesman trying to sell some kind of product." Jerome said. Sadie's cell phone rang. Jerome brought it to her, and she answered. "Hello?"

"Well, hello, Ms. Sadie. Forgot my voice already? This is your man, Eddie." Eddie chuckled.

"I don't want you to call me anymore. It's over!!!" Sadie said.

"Oh no baby, it has just begun." Eddie said with a laugh.

"Leave me alone!!!" Sadie yelled into the phone.

Jerome pleaded with her, "Sadie just hang up the phone. You don't have to talk to that joker. I am going to file a police report!!"

"Hey, I hear your man in the background. He really doesn't want to mess with me!! Did you forget!! I was going to make you a star. We were going to be rich, but you blew it, Sadie. Now you owe me, and I need you to pay up." Eddie explained.

"I don't owe you anything. I fell in love with you, and you hurt me. You hurt me physically, emotionally, and mentally. I am recovering and I am going to make it. I lost my baby, and I am really hurt about it, but I know God can heal my wounds. I don't need anybody like you. All you have done is cause me pain, and I want to be happy," Sadie cried.

"And I guess that dude makes you happy?" Eddie asked

"As a matter of fact, he does. He is a true friend and I trust him." Sadie responded.

Eddie was getting angry, "Girl, you don't want to make me mad because I will hurt you and him."

Sadie was not backing down, "You see, Eddie, you already hurt me, and I have taken all I can from you. I used to be afraid of you but now I am strong, and I can stand against anything. I want you to understand that it is over, and you need to go on with your life. I realize that I was naïve, and I let you into my life, but I know now that I made a big mistake. I have to learn to love myself before anyone else can love me."

"Oh, I see. You forgot where you came from. I was the one that took you off the streets and gave you a place to stay." Eddie reminded her.

"I wasn't on the streets!! I chose to leave my aunt's house because she had some issues. I was not on the streets so don't tell that lie anymore. If I had to go live at venus of hope downtown I would have done that, but you asked me to come and stay with you until I got on my feet. Now literally I am on my feet! Praise the Lord! I am going to make it. God gave me another chance and I am going to trust God to see me through. Now, just like I said before, don't call me, don't look for me, and don't think about me anymore. it is over!!" Sadie said with confidence as she hung up the phone.

"I didn't know that you had it in you. Girl, you told him!!" Jerome said with a smile.

"It was about time. I could not take him anymore. I realized that I have to go on with my life and make a change. You know that man was crazy!! I was a fool to fall in love with someone like that… you know what I mean?" Sadie asked.

"Um, Sadie? Look at you!!! You are walking!!!" Jerome said.

"Yes, I am!! I was so mad that I didn't notice that I was walking." Sadie said with joy.

God is really awesome!!" Jerome exclaimed.

"Yes, He is. We need to go to church tomorrow." Sadie said.

"Awe, I don't know. I haven't been to church in two years." Jerome said.

"Two years? Well, we are going to church Sunday. I want you to go to church with me." Sadie said.

Chapter 20

Sunday morning at 11:00a.m. Sadie and Jerome walked into Mt. Calvary Baptist Church. Rev. Ray was there. The choir was singing. So many memories began to flood Sadie's mind. She remembered when she was a little girl and her parents used to sit in the second pew. She remembered Sister Green who was still singing in the choir. Sister Green began to sing His Eye is on the Sparrow. The church was in a high praise. Sadie was happy and enjoying the service.

After the choir finished singing, Pastor Ray stood up and acknowledged the visitors.

"Good morning, church, now if we have any visitors please stand." Rev. Ray said.

Sadie shoved Jerome and they both stood up.

"Oh my Lord, I can't believe my eyes. Ms. Sadie Ward!!! Praise the Lord. Sadie, I know that you would like to have a word... you know what? Better than that come up here sister and give us a song." Rev. Ray said. The audience stood on their feet and gave Sadie a round of applause. "Come on Sister Ward we want to hear from you!!"

Sadie stood up slowly and walked up to the podium. She gave Pastor Ray a hug and also hugged Sister Green.

"Giving honor to God and to my pastor, Pastor Ray and the entire congregation," Sadie started to cry. "You all just don't know!! I am so glad to be able to come back home. When I walked into the church my mind began to think back to when I was a little girl coming to church with my parents. I used to sit right over there. I am so glad to be here. I've been through so much in the last five years that I just didn't think I was going to make it. My mother use to tell me that life will teach you and believe me that is a true statement. I have been through life's ups and downs but through it all I made it. There is one thing that I would like to share with the young women in this church. If you have a talent, make sure you use it for the Lord. Whatever talent it is, whether it is singing, praise dancing, writing, whatever it is use it for the Lord. Don't let the devil still your gift, your gift belong to the Lord."

The audience yelled out, "Testify. my sister."

Sadie continued, "I was trapped with the wrong people, and I was hurt really bad. I was so far gone that I forgot who I was. But I fell on my knees and cried out to the Lord. You know what? He heard my cry, and right now, today, I am back here at my home church singing for the Lord."

Sadie started singing, "As long as you keep your head to the sky... you can win." Everyone in the audience was standing up clapping and praising God. Jerome stood up and walked down the aisle to give his life to Christ. Sadie finished singing and Pastor Ray asked Jerome to have a word.

"Well, Pastor Ray, I have not been in church for two years. I was raised in the church, but church folks hurt me. Now I realize that it was not them, but it was me. I have to learn to trust God no matter what!!! Pastor, I know that this is probably not the appropriate time, but

I would like to say something to Sister Sadie." Pastor Ray motioned for him to continue. "Sadie. I know that you have been through a lot. I have been right there with you through it all. I want you to know that I have grown to love you and I am asking you to marry me." Jerome said with a smile. The audience started clapping.

"Yes, yes, I will marry you." Sadie says with excitement. The music starts again and Sadie sang.

Sadie and Jerome got married the following week.

Six months after their wedding, Jerome and Sadie were in church and Sadie was singing. Sissy walked into the church. She walked toward the podium, grabbed Sadie, and they hugged each other.

"Oh my god, Sissy I am surprised to see you." Sadie said.

"Sadie, I prayed that one-day you and I would meet you at the same place where we started. I am so glad we are in the house of God. I am drug free and I am starting a new life. I am going back to school to become a nurse. And did you hear? Eddie and Foster were arrested. They will be gone for a long time. Eddie was found guilty of attempted murder and possession of drugs. One of the main pieces of evidence was his Rolex that was found at the scene outside of the hospital. He was given ten years in prison and Foster was given five years for possession of drugs and managing a prostitution business. I can't believe we were ever caught up in all of that." Sissy said.

"I heard a little bit here and there, and the police asked me some questions, but I tried to stay away from it. Too many bad memories. I knew they were in prison. I hope that Eddie and Foster both have some time to think and change their ways." Sadie said.

"Oh, and I have another surprise for you," Sissy pointed towards the door. Aunt Neisse walked into the church with her new husband.

After the church service Aunt Neisse and Sadie reunited.

"Aunt Neisse, you look so good! What happen?" Sadie asked.

"Well, I decided to get myself together, go back to school, and get my master's degree. I've did some things that I am not proud of. I used to drink and get high almost every day. There's more, but I just want to keep it in my past. Any way, girl you are now looking at a new full-time lawyer." Aunt Neisse said with pride.

"Oh my god, Aunt Neisse I am so proud of you." Sadie hugged Aunt Neisse.

"Oh and I almost forgot, this is my husband Noel Robinson." Aunt Neisse smiled.

"How are you, Sadie? I've heard so many good things about you." Noel said.

Sadie could not stop smiling, "Oh Aunt Neisse, I am so glad we are all back together again."

Aunt Neisse and Sadie start singing together, "As long as you keep your head to the sky. you can win" .

Sadie became a professional gospel singer and recorded her first album with SOPFC Corporation. Even though Sadie was reared in a church environment and with a family with an educational background, that did not keep her from experiencing the trials and struggles of life. Yes, Sadie had a gift, a talent to share with others by exciting souls and spirits but who was there for Sadie when life threw a curve ball? Who was there when she lost something that is so precious to every woman in the world? Who was there when there was almost a chance of not being able to walk again? Yes, a gifted voice can make you happy, make you smile, and uplift for a moment, but who is there for the one who is sharing their gift?. One thing that must be realized by reading this book is that Sadie knew to keep her head to the sky... beyond the clouds, beyond the moon and the sun, there is a place call heaven. When I reach this place, I know that I can win…

the end…

Sadie

Written by: Cheryl Weams Lynn-Clay

Foreword

Cheryl Weams-Clay's book Sadie has a strong message for today.

The message that I received was to always keep my head to the sky because when I practice this, I know that I can win… keeping your head to the sky simply means: keep your eyes focused on God. Reading this book has taught me that while going through my trials and obstacles in life, I don't have to be defeated by the enemy. While going through experiences like Sadie went through, you have to keep God in your life. Several times Sadie had to fall on her knees and call on Jesus. That gave Sadie hope and faith to know that she would get the victory in the end. I cannot wait to read the next book that Cheryl Weams-Clay will write.

CPSIA information can be obtained
at www.ICGtesting.com
Printed in the USA
BVHW041416110422
633959BV00015B/724